Kaiden
the
Courageous
Beast

EBONY BLUE

It was a warm sunny day and Kaiden wanted to go to the park. As he had been thinking about how he wanted to get across the monkey bars without falling since his last trip to the park.

As he ran downstairs and burst into the kitchen,

he yelled mommy, mommy, can we go to the park? please please? Kaiden begged with excitement!

Of course we can, replied his mom, you and your brother go put your shoes on, and I'll get the car ready!

Kaiden was so excited, he could not sit still on the ride over to the park.

All he could think about was what it would feel like to finally cross to the other side of the monkey bars without falling, as he had always fallen down each time. Not this time. Kaiden was determined to finally reach the other side and he knew this time he would not give up.

As soon as they arrived at the park, both Kaiden and his brother un-buckled themselves and stormed out of the car.

While Kaiden's brother Josiah played on the slide, Kaiden ran straight to the monkey bars. As he glanced up at the shiny bars,

he took a deep breath, and began to climb the ladder, he exhaled and said to himself ok, I can do this! As he reached for the first bar and swung his legs and arms to reach for the second bar, he felt his hands start to slip and plop he fell to the ground,

Kaiden screamed OUCH, as his hands started to form blisters, his mom ran over and saw the blisters on his hands, asking was he ok, but she smiled and said your just building up tough skin, tough skin? Kaiden cried?

Yes, tough skin Kaiden's mom said. However, he didn't let that stop him he got back up shook his hands and said I will, and I can do this, with mighty confidence in his voice.

As he climbed the ladder again took a deep breath, he reached for the first bar than the second bar,

he fell again but kept getting back up. Kaiden's brother Josiah came over to see what his brother was doing and asked what are you doing? Kaiden just huffed and puffed

and said I'm trying to get across the monkey bars, but I keep falling Kaiden said in a sad tone

Josiah heard in his brother's voice how upset he sounded and said don't give up you just have to keep going. You can do it.

As Kaiden climbed the ladder, his mom yelled out five more minutes boys. His hands were burning, arms tired, and he was hot from the sun beaming down on him. Kaiden built his courage up and said to himself I can do this!

As his brother and a few other kids watched and cheered,

Kaiden swung his arm out to the first bar than the second he kept saying I will not give up, and before he knew it, he was on the other side of the monkey bars.

Kaiden felt a rush of joy and screamed I DID IT. I DID IT!

Kaiden felt so proud and so much joy and how he didn't give up. Kaiden had been working hard on the monkey bars. He finally did it.

On the ride home Kaiden told his mom and brother how happy he was. Yes Kaiden his mom replied Kaiden says I'm so proud of myself! Josiah and his mom both expressed how happy they were for him too!

END

To order additional copies of this book, contact:
Xlibris
844-714-8691
www.Xlibris.com
Orders@Xlibris.com

ISBN: Softcover   978-1-6698-2556-2
        Hardcover   978-1-6698-2557-9
        EBook   978-1-6698-2555-5

Print information available on the last page

Rev. date: 05/31/2022

Printed in the United States
by Baker & Taylor Publisher Services